World of the Drone

by

Robert Abernathy

World of the Drone
by Robert Abernathy

ISBN: 978-93-69074-52-5

Published by

DOUBLE 9 BOOKS

2/13-B, Ansari Road
Daryaganj, New Delhi – 110002
info@double9books.com
www.double9books.com
Tel. 011-40042856

ABOUT THE AUTHOR

Robert Abernathy was a prolific American science fiction author known for his thought-provoking narratives and insightful exploration of futuristic concepts. His masterpiece, "Hostage of Tomorrow," captivates readers with its gripping tale of a society held captive by its own technological advancements. Set in a dystopian future where humanity's dependence on technology has reached alarming heights, Abernathy weaves a compelling story of resistance and redemption. Through rich character development and intricate world-building, he paints a vivid picture of a world where individual freedoms are sacrificed at the altar of progress. "Hostage of Tomorrow" challenges readers to question the implications of unchecked technological growth and the ethical dilemmas that arise when humanity's pursuit of advancement threatens its very existence. Abernathy's masterful storytelling and keen insight into human nature elevate "Hostage of Tomorrow" beyond the confines of traditional science fiction, making it a timeless classic that continues to resonate with audiences today. With its blend of thrilling action, thought-provoking themes, and profound philosophical questions, Abernathy's "Hostage of Tomorrow" remains a must-read for fans of speculative fiction and dystopian literature alike.

CONTENTS

WORLD OF THE DRONE

The beetle woke from a dreamless sleep, yawned, stretched cramped limbs and smiled to himself. In the west the sunset's last glow faded. Stars sprang out in the clear desert sky, dimmed only by the white moon that rose full and brilliant above the eastern horizon.

Methodically, suppressing impatience, he went through every evening's ritual of waking. He checked his instruments, scanned the mirrors which gave him a broad view of moonlit desert to his left. To the right he could see nothing, for his little armored machine lay half-buried, burrowed deep into the sheltering flank of a great dune; all day long it had escaped the notice of prowling diurnal machines of prey. He listened, too, for any sound of danger which his amplifiers might pick up from near or far.

The motor, idling as it had all day while its master slept, responded to testing with a smooth, almost noiseless surge of power. The instruments were in order; there was plenty of water in the condenser, and though his food supply was low that shouldn't matter—before tonight was done he would be once more among his people.

Only the fuel gauge brought an impatient frown to his face. It was menacingly near the empty mark—which meant he would have to spend time foraging before he could continue his journey. Well ... no help for it. He opened the throttle.

The beetle's name was Dworn, and he was twenty-one years old. The flesh and blood of him, that is. The rest, the steel-armored shell, the wheels and engine and hydraulic power-system, the electric sensory equipment—all of which was to his mind as much part of his identity as his own skin, muscles, eyes and ears—was only five years old.

Dworn's face, under his sleep-tousled thatch of blond hair, was boyish. But there were hard lines of decision there, which the last months had left.... Tonight by the reckoning of his people, he was still a youth; but when tomorrow dawned, the testing of his wanderyear would be behind him, and he would be adult, a warrior of the beetle horde.

Sand spilled from the beetle's dull-black carapace as it surged from its hiding-place. It drifted, its motor only a murmur, along the shoulder of the dune. Dworn eyed his offending fuel gauge darkly; he would very much have liked to be on his way at top speed, toward the year's-end rendezvous of the horde under the shadow of the Barrier.

He began cruising slowly, at random, across the rolling moonlit waste of wind-built dunes, watching for spoor.

He spied, and swerved automatically to avoid, the cunningly concealed pit of a sand devil, strategically placed in a hollow of the ground. Cautiously Dworn circled back for a second look. The conical pit was partly fallen in, unrepaired; the devil was obviously gone.

The burrowing machine would, Dworn knew, have had fuel and other supplies somewhere in its deep lair, buried beneath the drifted sand where it spent its life breathing through a tube to the surface and waiting for unwary passers-by to skid into its trap. But Dworn regretfully concluded that it would not be worth while digging on the chance that whatever had done away with the devil had not rifled its stores.... He swung the beetle's nose about and accelerated again.

On the next rise, he paused to inspect the track of a pill-bug; but to his practiced eye it was quickly evident that the trail was too old, blowing sand had already blurred the mark of heels, and the bug probably was many miles away by now.

A mile farther on, luck smiled on him at last. He crossed the fresh and well-marked trail of a caterpillar—deeply indented tread-marks, meandering across the dunes.

He began following the spoor, still slowly, so as not to lose it or to run upon its maker unawares. A caterpillar was a lumbering monster of which he had no fear, but it was much bigger than a beetle, and could be dangerous when cornered. Dworn had no wish to corner it; the caterpillar itself was not the object of his stalking, but one of its supply caches which according to caterpillar custom it would have hidden at various places within its range.

The trail led him uphill, into a region cut by washes—dry now, since the rainy season was past—and by ridges that rose like naked vertebrae from the sea of sand that engulfed the valley floor.

Several times Dworn saw places where the caterpillar had halted, backed and filled, shoved piles of earth and rocks together or scraped patches of ground clear with its great shovel. But the beetle knew his prey's habits of old, and he passed by these spots without a second glance, aware that this conspicuous activity was no more than a ruse to deceive predators like himself. If Dworn hadn't known that trick, and many others used by the various non-predatory machine species which manufactured food and fuel by photosynthesis, he would have been unfit to be a beetle—and he would never have lived through the wanderyear which weeded out the unfit according to the beetle people's stern immemorial custom.

At last he came to a stop on a rocky hillside, where the tracks were faint and indistinct. Carefully scanning the ground downslope, he saw that his instinct had not misled him—the caterpillar had turned aside at this place and had afterward returned to its original trail, backing and dragging its digging-blade to obliterate the traces of its side excursion.

Dworn grinned, feeling the stirring of the hunter's excitement that never failed to move him, even on such a prosaic foraging expedition as this. He sent the beetle bumping down the slope.

The blurred trail led into the sandy bed of a wash at the foot of the hill, and along that easily-traveled way for a quarter mile. Then the stream made a sharp bend, undercutting a promontory on the left and creating a high bank of earth and soft white rock. Dworn saw that a section of the bank had collapsed and slid into the gully. That was no accident; the mark where a great blade had sheared into the overhang was plain to read, even if it had not been for the scuffed over vestiges of caterpillar tracks round about.

Dworn halted and listened intently, his amplifier turned all the way up. No sound broke the stillness, and the black moon-shadows within range of his vision did not stir.

He nosed the beetle carefully up to the heap. He had no equipment for moving those tons of soil and rock, but that was no matter. He twisted a knob on the control panel, a shutter in the beetle's forward cowling snapped open and a telescoping drill thrust from its housing, chattered briefly and took hold, while the engine's pulse strengthened to take up the load.

Twice Dworn abandoned fruitless borings and tried a different spot. On the third try, at almost full extension the drill-point screeched suddenly on metal and then as suddenly met no more resistance. Dworn switched on the pump, and quickly turned it off again; he swung the overhead hatch open, and—pausing to listen warily once more—clambered out onto the cowling, in the cold night air, to open the sample tap at the base of the drill and sniff the colorless fluid that trickled from it.

It gave off the potent odor of good fuel, and Dworn nodded to himself, not regretting his caution though in this case it had not been needed. But— clever caterpillars had been known to bury canisters of water in their caches, poison for the unsuspecting.

The pump throbbed again; there was the satisfying gurgle of fuel flowing into almost-empty tanks. Dworn leaned back, seizing the opportunity to relax for a moment in preparation for the strenuous journey still before him.

But he didn't fail to snap alert when just as the gauge trembled near the full mark, he heard pebbles rattling on the hillside above. Immediately thereupon he became aware of the grind of steel on stone and the rumbling of an imperfectly muffled engine.

In one smooth rapid motion Dworn switched off the pump, and spun the drill control. As the mechanism telescoped back into place, he gunned his engine, and the beetle shot backward and spun round to face the oncoming noise.

A squarish black silhouette loomed high on the slope above the overhanging bank, which rose so steeply that a stone loosened by turning treads bounded with a clang off the beetle's armor in the wash below. The caterpillar halted momentarily, engine grumbling to take in the scene.

Dworn didn't linger to learn its reaction at spying a looter. A snap shot from his turret gun exploded directly in front of the other machine, throwing up a cloud of dust and—he hoped—confusing its crew. And the beetle was fleeing around the bend in the stream bed, keeping close to the high bank.

A score of yards past the turning, intuition of danger made Dworn swerve sharply. An instant later, the ground blew up almost in his face—the bend had brought him into view, under the guns of the enemy above.

He wrenched the beetle around in a skidding turn and raced back for the bend where the overhang afforded shelter. Another shell and another crashed into places he had just left, and then he was safe—for the moment.

But it was an uncomfortable spot. The caterpillar rumbling wrathfully on the slope above him, couldn't see him as long as he hugged the bank, undercut by the water that flowed here in the rainy season; but, by the same token, he couldn't make a dash for safety without running the gauntlet of a murderous fire in the all-too-narrow way the stream bed offered. In open country, he would not have hesitated to count on his ability to outmaneuver and outshoot the caterpillar ... but here he was neatly trapped.

And it was nerve-racking to be unable to see what the enemy was about. It seemed to have halted, judging the situation just as he had been doing. Now, though, he heard its engine speed up again, and the grinding of its treads came unmistakably closer. His ears strained to gauge its advance as it came lurching down the slope, till it sounded only a few feet away and Dworn braced himself to shoot fast and straight if it started coming down over the bank. Then it paused again, and sat idling, hoping no doubt that he would panic and show himself.

He didn't. The caterpillar's engine raced up once more and began to labor under a heavy load. There was an increasing clatter of falling stones. Then Dworn remembered the great digging-blade it carried, and realized what it was going to try.

Ten feet to his right the bank began giving way. Tons of rubble thundered into the gully. Dworn winced and moved away as far as he dared. He heard the caterpillar back and turn, then it snarled with effort once more and another section of the overhang caved in with a grinding roar.

Inside minutes at this rate, it would either have driven him from his refuge or buried him alive. Now it came rumbling forward for the third time; rocks showered from the rim directly above his head, and he saw the bank begin to tremble.

Dworn braced himself. Even as the wall of earth and rock began leaning outward above him, he gave his engine full throttle. The wheels spun for one sickening instant, then the little machine lunged forward from beneath the fresh landslide and was climbing, bucking and slewing, up the slope of loose soil created by the ones before.

The caterpillar loomed black and enormous on his left hand, so close that it could not have brought its guns to bear even if its crew had expected the beetle to take this daring way out. With its shovel lowered and half-buried, it could not swing round quickly—Dworn had counted on that.

As the beetle's flank cleared the corner of the digging blade with inches to spare, Dworn's gun turret passed in line with the space between the blade and the caterpillar's treads, and he jabbed the firing button. The explosion wreathed the monster's forward half in smoke and dust, and into that cloud it tilted forward, teetered ponderously and then slid headlong to the bottom of the wash as the loosened bank gave way conclusively under its great weight.

Dworn looked back from the hill crest to see it still floundering, treads furiously churning sand, struggling to fight clear of the avalanche it had carried with it. The beetle laughed full-throatedly, without rancor. This hadn't been the first nor the tightest corner he'd been in during the dangerous course of his wanderyear; and in that hard school of life you learned not to worry about danger already past.

At another time, he might have returned to the battle in hope of capturing the additional supplies the caterpillar carried and—still more valuable booty—the chart it would have, showing the location of its other caches. But now he was in a hurry—this refueling foray had cost him a couple of hours, and the moon was already high.

So he slipped quietly away over the ridge and set his course to the east.

Beyond the hilly land, the terrain ironed out into level alkali flats where a vanished lake had been in the long-gone days when the earth was fertile. There he opened the throttle wide. The plain, white in the moonlight, rolled under the racing wheels at ninety and a hundred miles an hour; air whistled over the carapace....

Impatience surged up in Dworn once more. Eagerly he pictured his forthcoming reunion with his native horde—and with Yold, his father, chief of the horde.

Countless times in the long wanderyear—in moments when death loomed nearer than it had in the brush just past, and he despaired of surviving his testing, or in other moments, yet harder to bear, when the immensity of of the desert earth seemed about to swallow him up in his loneliness—he had grasped at that vision now soon to be real: he, Dworn, stood before the assembled horde, the year of his proving triumphantly completed, and he received before them all the proud, laconic commendation of the chief, his father.

Hungrily he scanned the horizon ahead, saw with leaping heart that it was no longer flat. Along it a black line rose, and grew ragged as it came nearer, and became an endless line of cliffs, marching straight north and south as far as the eye could see.... The Barrier!

Dworn recognized familiar landmarks, and altered his direction a little so as to be heading directly for the year's-end rendezvous. He knew, from childhood memories even, the outline of that vast stone rampart as it appeared by moonlight. Every year the Barrier formed the eastern limit of the beetles' annual migration, as naturally as the shore of the sea was its westward terminus. So it had been for a thousand years or more, as far back as the oldest traditions reached: generation after generation, hunting, foraging, and fighting—from the Barrier to the ocean, from the ocean to the Barrier.

To right and left the serried cliffs stretched out of sight—the edge of the world, so far as beetles knew. If you examined the contour of its rim, you could see how it corresponded point by point to the irregularities of the hilly land on its hither side. Some time, millennia ago, a great fault in the earth's crust had given way, and the unknown lands of the continental interior had been lifted as if on a platform, five hundred feet above the coastal regions. Or perhaps the coast had sunk. Legend attributed the event to the ancients' wars, when, it was said, some unimaginable weapon had cleft the continent asunder....

Dworn perforce slowed his breakneck pace as the ground grew uneven again. He guided his machine with instinctive skill over the ascending slopes and ridges, eyes combing the moon-shadows for the first sign of his people.

Then, a couple of miles ahead, he glimpsed lights. His heart bounded up—then sank with a prescient dismay; there was something wrong—

The fires that winked up there—four, no, five of them, under the very rim just before the cliffs rose sheer—didn't look like campfires. They were unequally spaced, and they flared up and waned oddly by turns, glowing evilly red.

Dworn braked the beetle to a stop on a patch of high ground, and sat straining to discern the meaning of those ominous beacons. To his imagination, rasped raw by expectation and the tension of long travel, they became red eyes of menace, warnings.... He tried the infrared viewer, but it showed no more than he could see with the naked eye. Only ghosts paraded across the screen, ghosts of the folded slopes that rose to the abrupt wall of the Barrier. Nothing seemed moving there; the whole sweep of broken and tumbled landscape appeared dead and lifeless as the moon.

But yonder burned the fires.

Sternly Dworn reminded himself that this night he was mature, a warrior of the proud beetle race. He thrust his fears resolutely aside; there was nothing to do but find out.

The beetle drifted forward, but cautiously now, at a stalking pace. Dworn took advantage of the lie of the land, continually seeking cover as he advanced, to shield him from whatever eyes might be watching from the silent slopes above.

Boulders lay ever more thickly strewn as he neared the Barrier cliffs, and he skirted patches of gravel and loose stones that would have crunched loudly under his wheels. Only occasionally, emerging into the open, he glimpsed his objective, but his sense of direction kept him bearing steadily toward the fires.

Fifteen minutes later, the beetle's blunt nose thrusting from under a shelf of rock that would disguise its outline if anything was watching, its motor noiselessly idling, Dworn knew that his premonitions had not been in vain. He looked out upon a scene that chilled his blood.

The burning machines, scattered for two hundred yards along the talus slope where destruction had come upon them or where they had plunged out of control, were beetles. Or they had been. Now they were wrecks, smashed, overturned, fitfully aflame.

There was no sign of an enemy. But here was the havoc which some powerful enemy had wrought, it could not have been long ago.

He strove to find identifying marks on the blackened hulks, but in the uncertain light could make out at first no more than the female ornaments which had graced two or three of them. Names and faces flashed through Dworn's mind; he could not know yet who had perished here, which faces he would not see again....

It hardly occurred to him to speculate that anyone might be left alive on the scene of the debacle. For one thing, the destruction's thoroughness was too evident, and besides, in Dworn's mind, by all his background and his teaching, human and machine were inextricably one; when one perished, so did the other....

There was a dull explosion, a shower of sparks and a spreading glare as a fuel tank blew up. The flare revealed the pillar of smoke, blood-colored by reflection, that towered into the night above the scene.

And it revealed more. For Dworn saw by that unholy light that one of the nearer beetles—capsized and burned out, its carapace burst raggedly open—it bore the golden scarab emblem which was the chief's alone.

The sight smote Dworn like a physical blow, so that he almost cried out aloud. Somehow it had not even crossed his mind that his father Yold could have been among the slain in whatever disaster had fallen upon the beetles here.... Others might die; but his father was a pillar of strength that could not fall—the grave iron-willed chief, demanding and rewarding, for his son impartially as for all the people....

Dworn's breath choked in his throat and his eyes stung. Fiercely he told himself that a beetle, a chief's son, did not weep.

Not to mourn—to revenge, that was his duty. By the law of his people, the bereaved son must seek out and slay not less than three members of whatever race had done his father to death. Until then, his father's insatiate spirit would roam the deserts without rest....

But Dworn did not even know as yet who had done this night's work.

Suddenly, by the new blaze that still continued, he saw movement, a dull sheen of metal moving, and he froze the gesture that had been about to send him forward into the arena of death.

The infrared was useless; by it the flickering firelight was blinding. Dworn bit his lip in anger at his own lack of precaution, and hastily twisted his sound-receptor control to maximum. The crackling of the flames swelled to a hissing roar, but through it he heard the unmistakable creaking sound of treads. Beyond the smoke moved an indistinct and monstrous shape.

Dworn's jaw muscles set rock-hard and his hand flashed to another control. His turret gun revolved soundlessly, and the crosshairs of the sight danced across the mirrored image of the approaching thing. His finger poised over the firing button, he braced himself to fling his machine into swift evasive action before the enemy's perhaps overwhelming firepower could reply—

The monster lumbered slowly into the light, canted far over and traveling with an odd sidling motion along the steep rubbly slope. Great treads set far out on each side of the squat, ungainly body preserved it against overturning. Its flattened forward turret swiveled nervously from side to side, peering blackly from vision ports steel-shuttered down to squinting slits.

And Dworn relaxed. The red hatred that had blazed up in him subsided into mere disgust; he watched the great machine's wary progress with a familiar, instinctive contempt. It was a scavenger, huge but not very formidable, drawn from afar by the fires which promised loot, salvageable scrap, perhaps even usable parts, fuel or ammunition.... It could not possibly have been responsible for the carnage; such cowardly creatures gave a wide berth to the beetle horde.

The monster ground to a halt amid the wreckage. Then its engine bellowed with sudden power and it spun half round, one tread spraying gravel, and backed hastily away up the slope. And Dworn was aware that the noise of creaking treads had redoubled. He cast about, and saw, laboring upward from below, another big machine, closely similar to the first.

Both scavengers came to a stop, facing one another across the fading of the fires, their unmuffled engines grumbling sullenly. Dworn watched them narrowly, expecting the shooting to begin any moment. But the scavengers' way of life was not one that encouraged reckless valor. After a long minute, a hatch-cover was lifted in the first arrival's armored back; a cautious head thrust forth, and shouted hoarsely, words clear to Dworn's amplified hearing:

"Better go back where you came from, brother. We got here first!"

The other scavenger's turret-hatch also swung slightly open. A different voice answered: "Don't talk foolishness, brother. We've got as much right here as you, and anyway we *saw* it first!"

The first voice thickened with belligerence. "We've got the advantage of the ground on you, brother. Better back up!"

"Oh, go smelt pebbles!" snarled the other. No doubt that was a scathing rejoinder among the scavengers.

Dworn grimaced scornfully and brought his turret-gun to bear on an outcropping midway between the disputants. Either of them outweighed the little beetle twenty times over—but at this juncture a single unexpected shot would probably send both of them scuttling for cover—

But he halted again on the verge of firing. For he had not stopped listening, and now his trained ears picked out another, an unfamiliar sound from the background of noises.

It was a queer rattle and scurry, mingled with a high-pitched buzz that could only come from a number of small but high-speed motors. It was not a sound the exact like of which Dworn remembered having heard before. He went rigid, staring, as the sound's source came into view.

A column of little machines—lighter even than a beetle, and more elongated—advancing in single file, multiple wheels swerving in the leader's tracks as the column wound nearer along the mountainside. As the firelight fell on them they gleamed with the mild sheen of aluminum. Round vision-ports stared glassily, and turbines buzzed feverishly shrill.

With astonishing bravado, the flimsy little vehicles, one behind another, came parading onto the wreck-strewn slope.

And what was more startling still—no two of them were alike. The leader mounted a winch in plain view; behind came another machine fitted with oddly-shaped grappling claws, and next one bearing a mysterious device terminating in front in a sort of flexible trunk.... Strangely, too, they didn't seem to carry any armament—no snouting guns, no flame or gas projectors.

Despite that fact or perhaps because of it, something sounded an alarm deep in Dworn's mind.

Their diversity itself was uncanny, that was certain. In all Dworn's experience, machines were the work of races whose traditions of construction, handed down from forgotten antiquity, were as fixed and unvarying as the biological heredity that made one race light-haired, another dark....

A hatch-cover clanged shut, and another. The squabbling scavengers had finally noticed the appearance of outside competition. The one upslope raced its engine uncertainly, swung round to face the buzzing invaders, hesitated.

The newcomers, for their part, seemed oblivious to the scavengers' presence. Their column began dispersing. A grapple-armed machine laid hold on one of the wrecked beetles and, whining with effort, sought to drag it to leveler ground. A second, following, spat a burst of sparks and extended a gleaming arm tipped by the singing blue radiance of a cutting torch.

The first-come scavenger growled throatily and lumbered toward the interlopers, plainly taking heart from their air of harmless stupidity. Behind it, the other scavenger came clattering up the slope to its fellow's aid.

Flame bloomed thunderously from the muzzle of the first one's forward gun. The machine with the torch was flung bodily into the air and went rolling and bouncing down the hill, wheels futilely spinning. The gun roared again, and the exploding shell tore open a flimsy aluminum body from nose to tail. Motors whirred frantically as the pygmies scattered before the charging behemoth. One of them darted witlessly right under the huge treads, and disappeared with a brief screech of crumpling metal.

The fight was over as quickly as it had begun. The scavenger wheeled, snorting, and fired one more shot into the dark after its routed opponents....

Dworn muttered an imprecation under his breath. No chance of frightening the scavengers off now that their blood was up and their differences forgotten; and a lone beetle could scarcely stand up to two of them in a knock down fight. To rush in now would be suicidal.

He gave up the idea of investigating the scene of disaster more closely, and backed stealthily away, keeping to the cover of the rocks. At a safe distance he began circling round, downslope.

What he could and must do now was to locate what was left of his native horde. It had numbered about fifty when he had departed for his wanderyear; a dozen, perhaps more, had died on the mountain tonight. He must seek out the survivors, and help plan retaliation against whatever enemy had dealt them this terrible blow.

Yet something else nagged at his mind, until he halted to gaze achingly once more toward the glowing embers up there, where the scavengers now clanked to and fro about their business.

Dworn recognized that what bothered him was the puzzle of the unidentified little machines that had turned up on the battlefield only to be sent packing. During his yearlong solitary struggle to survive, he had developed an extra sense or two—and in the queerly confident behavior of those buzzing strangers he had scented danger, a trap....

So it happened that he was still looking on at the moment when the trap was sprung.

A star, it seemed, fell almost vertically from the zenith, falling and expanding with the uncanny silence of flight faster than sound. The scavengers had no time to act. Dworn caught one faint glimpse of a winged shape against the sky, limned by the flashes that stabbed from it as it leveled out of its terrific dive.

One scavenger shuddered with the force of a heavy explosion somewhere within it, and subsided, smoking. The other too staggered under crippling impacts, but ground somehow into motion, spinning and sliding crazily down the gravel slope. Then, as the first attacker's shock-wave made the very earth tremble, a second and a third plunged from the black heights, and as the last one rose screeching from its swoop the whole lower face of the hillside boomed into a holocaust of flame and oily smoke. The fleeing scavenger was gone, enveloped somewhere in an acre of fiery hell.

Dworn, two hundred yards away, felt a searing breath of heat, and with a great effort controlled the impulse to whirl round and race for opener ground. He sat still, hands cramped sweating on the beetle's controls, while the sky whistled vindictively with the flight of things that circled in search of further targets.

When, after a seeming eon, their screaming died away, he released held breath in a long sigh. He found himself trembling with reaction. Still he didn't stir. He was ransacking his memory for something he should be able to recall but which eluded him—a myth, perhaps, heard as a child beside the campfires of the horde—

The old men would know; Yold would have known. At thought of his father, the grief and fury rose up again in Dworn, and this time he knew the object of his vengeful anger. There was small doubt now in his mind that those flying machines which struck so swiftly and so murderously had been the beetles' attackers.

But he didn't know what they were. He knew, of course, about the machines called hornets, which could fly and strike at fearful speeds like that, outracing sound. But the hornets flew only in daylight, and made no trouble for the nocturnal race of beetles. These—were something else.

And more—between the deadly night-fliers and the harmless-looking aluminum crawlers he had seen, Dworn sensed some connection, some unnatured symbiosis. He had heard vague rumors about such arrangements, but had half-discounted them; any of the peoples whom he knew at first hand would have scorned to enter into alliance with an alien species.

Lastly, he realized bitterly, he didn't even know where the enemy's lair, their base on the ground, might be....

The moon stood high now. But the Barrier, close at hand now, rose like an immense black wall, folded in shadows, revealing no secrets—walling off the world the beetles knew from the unknown beyond. Involuntarily Dworn shivered. He couldn't be sure—but it seemed to him that the destroyers had come from over the Barrier and had flown back there.

He set his machine in cautious motion again and stole along, making northward and keeping close to the Barrier. It occurred to him that the beetle horde, routed and fleeing, might well have hugged the cliffs for protection against flying foes.

The going here was not easy. The terrain seemed increasingly unfamiliar though he should have known every foot of it. But—he remembered no such tumbled crags, no such great heaps of stony detritus as blocked his way and forced him into long detours....

Finally he halted to take his bearings, and, looking up, discovered what had happened. The black rampart of the Barrier was notched and broken. Sometime in the past year, since Dworn had left this place to begin his wandering, a quarter-mile-wide section of the upper crags, hollowed and loosened by the slow working of millennial erosion, had fallen and spilled millions of tons of rock crashing and shattering onto the slopes below. Here now water would run when the rains fell, and in ten or twenty thousand years, perhaps, a river-course would have completed the breach.

Dworn wondered fleetingly whether any living thing had been here when the cliffs fell. If so, it was buried now, crumbling bone and corroding metal, under the mountain for all time to come.

He set about skirting the rockfall, still searching the ground for traces of beetle wheels. But there were very few wheel or tread marks of any description to be seen—and that was strange in itself.

Impulsively he halted again and listened, his amplifier turned up. He should have heard faroff engine-mutterings, occasional explosions from the desert to the west, where normally the predatory machines and their victims prowled and fought all night long over the sandy tracts and the desolate ridges.... But there was nothing. A silence, vast and unnatural, lay upon the wastes in the shadow of the high plateau.

He looked up again at the fallen rampart of the Barrier. The great landship had opened, as it were, a gateway to the unknown lands in the east—a gateway for what?

There was a strangeness here since last year, and the strangeness crept chillingly into Dworn's blood, made the mountain air seem thin and cold.

As he started again, he noticed yet another curious thing. He was crossing a sandy natural terrace, and the soft soil here was traversed by a row of indented marks that marched in a straight line across the open space. They were scuffed depressions, such as a ricocheting projectile might have made—but oddly regular in shape and spacing, almost, he thought fancifully, like giant footprints, ten feet apart....

Dworn was growing numbed to riddles. He shrugged impatiently and pressed the accelerator again.

He would push on northward for a few more miles, he determined, and if he still found no sign of his people, he would circle back to the south....

The moonlight shadow of the huge tilted boulder ahead was inky. But Dworn was keeping to the shadows by preference, remembering the death from above; so he cut close around the overhanging rock.

Too late to swerve, then, he saw the gleam of something stretched across his path. A metallic glint of deceptively slender strands which, as the beetle rolled headlong into them, snapped taut without breaking, sprang back and flipped the beetle clean over to fetch up against the rock with an ear-shattering bang.

Half-stunned by the suddenness of it and the violence with which he had been flung about, Dworn blurrily saw other cables settling from overhead, coiling almost like living things around his overturned machine. Then he glimpsed something else; stalking monstrously down from the unscalable crag above, its armor glimmering in the moonlight, a machine such as he had never imagined—a machine without wheels or treads, a nightmare moving on jointed steel legs that flexed and found holds for clawed steel feet with the smooth precision of well-oiled pistons. A machine that walked.

Capsized, its vulnerable underside exposed, the beetle was all but helpless. One hope remained. With wooden fingers Dworn groped for the emergency button, found it—

The propellant-charge went off beneath him with a deafening roar. The beetle was hurled upward and sidewise, in an arc that should have brought it down on its wheels again—but the ensnaring cables tightened and held, and Dworn's head slammed against something inside the cabin. The world burst apart into a shower of lights and darkness....

Dworn came awake to a pounding head and blurred light in his eyes. He moved, and sensed that he was bound.

His vision cleared. He saw that he was in a closed, half-darkened chamber—and that discovery alone made him shudder, he who as a free beetle had spent his whole life under desert skies. His feet rested on a floor of hard-packed sand, and his back, behind which his wrists were lashed together was propped uncomfortably against a wall ribbed with metal girders. The room was circular and its walls converged upward, into tangled shadows overhead; the chamber was roughly bottle-shaped.

To one side a door stood ajar, and it was thence that the light streamed, but from where he was Dworn couldn't see into the space beyond.

He tried hard to collect his thoughts. When had everything stopped making sense? When he had first glimpsed the fires that were burning beetles on the mountainside, or....

The converging lines of the wall-girders led his eyes upward. The shadows overhead resolved themselves as he studied them, and Dworn's heart pounded as he commenced to understand what manner of place he was in. The roof of the bottle-shaped chamber—he was sure it must be underground—was no roof, but was the underside of a great machine complex with gear-housings and levers connected with the six powerful metal legs radiating from it, their cleated feet resting on a shelf that encircled the bottle-neck. It squatted there, motionless above him, sealing the entrance to its burrow....

Trapped. For some reason he couldn't guess at, he had been taken alive—his human body, at least; he didn't know what had become of the rest of him, the machine that was part and parcel of him too.

The light suddenly brightened. The door at one side was swinging open.

Dworn blinked at the glare from the lighted room beyond. Against it a figure stood in silhouette, and he saw that it was a woman.

She was slender, not very tall, and her hair was jet-black, a striking frame for a startlingly pale face. Here beneath the earth she must not get much sun.... In that white face her lips were shockingly red, the color of fresh blood. And the nails of her slim white fingers were crimson claws. After a moment, he realized that both must be painted—a strange thing to him, for there was no such practice among beetle women.

She was clad in a coverall suit of much the same design as the green garment Dworn wore according to beetle custom. But her garb was shiny black, and in front, between the swelling mounds of her breasts, was an emblem he did not understand; the shape of an hourglass, in vermilion red.

She stood gazing at him, smiling a little with a curve of scarlet lips that revealed white, sharp-looking teeth. Dworn groped for his voice; but she spoke first.

"Patience, beetle," she said. "I'll attend to you in a moment."

The words had the accent of a strange speech, but they were intelligible. Dworn stared uncomprehendingly at her, mumbled, "Who—*what* are you?"

She moved nearer and stood smiling down at him. "Why, beetle, don't you know?... I'm the spider who caught you."

"*Spi-der?*" Dworn fumbled with the unfamiliar word. "I don't—"

Her eyes too were black, very black and intense. She said slowly, "You don't know about spiders, beetle? Strange. It must be that till now there were none of our kind on this side of the Rim."

Dworn's aching head was not serving him well, but a part of his intelligence functioned to grapple with the implication of her words. "The Rim"—that must mean the Barrier, as seen from its eastern side. Then she, and others like her, must have come from beyond the Barrier. A walking machine could descend by the broken path of the landslide.

But "spider"—the word rang some bell deep in his mind, some recollection of childhood's fairytale bogeys perhaps, but he still hadn't succeeded in grasping the memory.

He growled, "I don't know—but if you'd untie my hands, I'd show you what a beetle is."

She eyed him thoughtfully. Then she smiled, showing the sharp little white teeth again. "Presently I'll free you. When it's quite safe. As soon as—" Her hand dipped to a small black case secured to her belt, and came up with a diminutive gleaming object—a slender needle thrusting from a liquid-filled plastic cylinder fitted with a plunger. "Do you know what *this* is, beetle?"

Dworn glowered silently.

"When I've injected this fluid into your veins, you will have no will of your own left. You'll do what I say, and only what I say—for the rest of your life, beetle!"

Dworn's eyes clung in unwilling fascination to the glittering needle. He said through stiff lips, "Now I remember. Your kind is a legend among my people. The evil women who have no men ... who kill their male children at birth, and trap their mates from among the other races, and kill them, too, when they no longer want them.... *Spider!*"

His gaze collided squarely with hers, and she needed no skill to read the loathing in it, rendered more violent by her beauty that he could not help but see.

Her eyes dropped first. She clutched the needle and muttered fiercely to herself, "But when you've had the injection, it won't matter. I'll say, 'Love me!' and you'll love me, and 'Die!' and you'll die...."

Dworn stared burningly at the slim figure in black with the scarlet hourglass on her bosom. He was alert again, and his mind was racing. To all appearances he was lost—but something in the spider girl's manner gave him an unreasonable hope.

He said abruptly, "So. Why didn't you use your poison while I was stunned? That would have been easy."

She looked away. "You ask foolish questions, beetle. Naturally, I had to prepare myself according to our customs. I had to paint my face and make myself beautiful...."

He said inspiredly, "You *are* beautiful."

Her reaction was surprising. She stood gazing raptly at him, lips slightly parted the hypodermic forgotten in her hand. Dworn sensed that had he been unbound, he would have had no trouble overpowering her.

She whispered, "*It's true, then!*"

And he realized forcibly how young she was—the painted lips made her look much older, and the shadows—which he now saw were also painted on—beneath her eyes. Only a girl, and if she had been one of his own people he would have looked at her twice and more than twice....

But above their heads the great spider-machine's underparts gleamed dully, straddling the sunken den. And the spell lasted only a moment.

The girl straightened her shoulders and took a deep breath. "Why am I talking to a beetle? It's time—"

There was a clang of metal from somewhere in the room beyond. The girl's face reflected sudden fright, beneath its painted mask. She spun round and took two steps toward the inner door, but even as she did so, the door swung wide, and dark figures crowded through it.

The girl cried, with terror and anger in her voice, "What do you mean, coming into my Nest like this? You have no right—"

The interlopers were three in number, and all of them were women, wearing black garments like the girl's, with the red spider symbol on the breast. The one in the lead was elderly, her hair wisped with gray, and her face was lined by years and passions; her eyes were flinty, her mouth thin and cruel. The other two were younger; one was a strapping blonde wench taller than Dworn, who moved with a powerful and formidable grace; the other was short, soft-looking, with a child's pouting mouth and a queer, mad glint in her dark eyes.

The older woman said, "No right? You've had your own Nest for all of three months now, dear Qanya, and already you tell your Mother that she has no right to enter?"

The girl quailed. She retreated step by step until her back was against the wall beside Dworn, and met the old woman's eyes with a look half fright, half defiance.

"But, of course, you have your reasons," the Spider Mother went on bitingly. Her hard eyes stabbed at the bound and helpless Dworn. "Somewhere you managed to catch this, and bring him in without letting anyone know, and paint your face and prepare the needle.... You chose to forget that in times like these there are others of the Family whose claim to a mate has priority over yours!"

"*That's* true, Mother!" said the tall blonde energetically. The plump girl licked her full lips and said nothing.

"Quiet, Purri!" snapped the Spider Mother. Her eyes raked the girl Qanya again. "Well, and what do you have to say for yourself?"

Qanya's black eyes flashed. "I caught him myself," she blazed. "You've no right—"

"No right, no right," mocked the old woman. "Why, I believe that, if you'd dared, you'd have blocked up the connecting tunnel so we couldn't walk in on you. Who has rights is for *me* to decide—and for me to decide whether you're whipped and sent back to the young girls' dormitory. Until I've made up my mind—" She turned and frowned thoughtfully at her two companions, jabbed a finger at the tall one. "You, Purri, stay here and see that nothing happens to the catch, and make sure our little Qanya doesn't misbehave. I'm going to my Nest and check over the Family ledger, to settle the question of who's first in line for a mate. We've got to be strict, now that the cursed night-fliers are everywhere and it's been so long since we trapped a presentable male." She eyed Dworn once more, and smiled thinly. "He's a fine youth. Who knows? I might even take him for myself."

Dworn had no stomach for the compliment. Secretly, he was twisting his bound hands behind him, trying to loosen the knots. Those knots had been none too skillfully tied, and given time.... But he had to desist as the tall Purri strode near and stood over him. She cast a glance after the retreating backs of the Spider Mother and her other proteges, then devoted all her attention to Dworn, surveying him in critical silence and with a business-like eye for detail.

Qanya huddled against the wall; her dark eyes were enormous, and tears had streaked the make-up on her cheeks.

Purri nodded satisfiedly. "He'll do," she said matter-of-factly to Qanya. "The Mother should give him to me. It's a choice between me and Marza, really—" She jerked her head toward the door through which the dark, pouting girl had gone—"But Marza doesn't really appreciate a mate. All she cares about is seeing how long she can take to make them die."

Qanya stared hotly at her. She said in a stifled voice, "You're a beast, and Marza is a beast, and—"

"Careful!" said Purri lazily. "If you say anything against the Mother, I'll have to report you." Arms akimbo, she looked scornfully down at the younger girl's tearful face.

Dworn had been right about the knots Qanya had tied. They were slipping. He wrestled in silence, hoping for a little more time.... Then he was sickeningly aware that Qanya was looking toward him, had seen what he was doing. For an instant he froze.

Qanya said hurriedly, "Anyway, *you're* a beast, Purri. A greedy one. You've had two mates already—why didn't you make them last? And I've not even had one."

"When you're older," said Purri loftily, her back still turned to the struggling beetle, "you'll understand more. But you ought to know from your schooling that there are some races that mate for life—and among them, the males dominate the female. We spiders are above such degrading practices."

Qanya's eyes flicked momentarily to Dworn, who was wrenching at the final knot. "Yes, yes, I know," she said. "But I still say it isn't fair—"

Dworn came catlike to his feet, ignoring the pain of cramped limbs. The cord with which he had been bound was looped in his hands. With a single stride he was upon the unwarned Purri; one hand clamped over her mouth, cutting off outcry, and the other hand whipped the cord tight around her. She fought with the strength of a man, but futilely. Dworn ripped a length of fabric from her clothing and improvised a gag; when he was done, the spider woman could do no more than kick and gurgle a little.

During the brief struggle, Qanya had watched without making a sound, hands pressed against the girdered wall at her back. As Dworn faced her now, breathing hard, he saw fear written large in her face.

She whispered, "Beetle, you won't hurt me?"

Dworn hesitated briefly. There was no doubt she had helped him—if only out of jealousy of the others. But at the same time she was a spider, a natural enemy. And time was desperately vital. In a flash of inspiration, he saw that there was one way to make sure of his escape.

"If you're quiet," he promised, "I won't hurt you. Not much, anyway." Then his arm was about her, pinioning her, while his free hand snaked to her waist and plucked the hypodermic from its case. For a moment she struggled and even tried to bite him, as she saw what he was about to do. Then, clumsily but effectively, he had stabbed the needle into her upper arm and pressed the plunger home.

He felt her stiffen and then relax, shivering, as the drug coursed through her blood. He released her and stepped back, watching her warily.

"How do you like your own medicine, spider?" he demanded harshly.

The girl stood motionless. Her black eyes, fixed on him, seemed to dull as if with sleep.

"Do you hear me?"

"Yes," she said tonelessly.

"Do you obey me if I give you orders?"

"Yes."

Dworn grinned exultantly. It had worked—But there was no time to lose. The Spider Mother might return any moment.

"Where is my machine?"

She answered without expression, "I left it where it was. I didn't want it, I was only seeking a mate."

Dworn sighed with heartfelt relief. He looked upward, toward the spider-machine overhead: "All right. I command you to take me back to the place where you left my beetle."

Qanya turned silently toward a slender steel ladder that rose to the belly of the crouching metal monster. Dworn followed her, his nerves still strung close to the snapping point, but with hope leaping in him.... On the floor, the trussed-up Purri stared up with round eyes and made smothered noises.

They clambered into the spider through a port in its underside, past the engines and the great drums of steel cable which served to snare the spider's prey. The space within was cramped, barely big enough to hold two, and its instruments and controls were bewilderingly strange to Dworn. The tangle of switches and levers that must govern the mechanical legs made no sense at all to him, and he felt a moment of near-panic: if the hypnotic injection's magic should fail, he would be quite helpless here.

Braving it out, he snapped, "Make it go!"

Obediently Qanya touched this and that control. The spider's engine throbbed with power, and its legs straightened, lifting it so quickly as to cause a sinking sensation in the stomach. From overhead came a creaking, and a band of light appeared and widened, grew dazzling as a circular trapdoor opened on daylight.

Dworn caught his breath. He hadn't reckoned with its being daytime; evidently he had been unconscious longer than he had supposed. But he couldn't worry about that.

"Go on!" he rasped. "Outside!"

The machine clambered stiffly out of its burrow; sand crunched under its steel feet. Blinking at the sun, Dworn saw that the trap opened on a stretch of boulder-strewn wasteland; it must not be far from the foot of the great slide. The trapdoor was coated with sand to make it appear only a half-buried rock, and in the near distance were other, closely similar outcroppings that were very likely the entrances to other spiders' burrows.

"Get us away from here! Quick!" ordered Dworn shakily.

Still wordlessly, her face smooth and mask-like, the girl set the walking machine in motion. It moved with a queer rolling gait which made Dworn dizzy, though it stilted over the irregularities of the ground with scarcely a jar. Dworn felt nakedly exposed, riding high above the ground in broad daylight, but he gritted his teeth and tried not to think of the probability of attack by some day-faring marauder. He supposed the spider girl, accustomed likewise to a nocturnal life, would have felt the same fear of the light, if she hadn't been hypnotized.

Under the drug's influence she apparently couldn't speak unless spoken to. However, there were questions he wanted to ask her.

First—"What do you know about the attack on the beetles last night?"

"I know there was a battle," said Qanya flatly, without looking up from the controls. "I didn't see it, but the Mother and some others were prowling at the time, and saw. It was the flying things, which have given us too so much trouble."

That, if true—and he judged that it *must* be true—confirmed his prior suspicion, and killed another suspicion he had entertained for a little while— that the spiders themselves might have been the ambushers. He demanded, "What do you know about those night-fliers?"

"Very little. We do not know just what they are or where they came from. They began appearing hereabouts only four months ago, which was three months after the Rim collapsed and the Mother decided that we should descend and try the hunting on this side. Since then they've grown more and more numerous. They fly by day as well as by night, and attack everything that moves. They've taken several of our Family, and I think they've made heavy depredations on the peoples that inhabit this region. We spiders would have abandoned the location before now, but we feared to be caught migrating in the open...."

Dworn gazed apprehensively out at the glaring desert that was rolling past the spider windows. The news that the aerial killers also operated by day was most unwelcome. But as yet there was no sign of an enemy.

He said, "The little ground machines—unarmored, made of aluminum. They're allied in some way to the flying ones, aren't they?"

"We think so. Wherever the flying machines have made a kill, the crawlers appear before long to carry away the spoils. And if they're attacked—the fliers come swooping down within minutes to defend or avenge them. So most of the other inhabitants have learned to leave the crawlers alone; it's extremely dangerous to meddle with them."

Dworn could confirm that fact from his own observation.

Evidently the spider folk, even though they came from beyond the Barrier as the mysterious others apparently had too, knew little more than he himself had already discovered. But—there was one more question.

"Do you know," he asked tensely, "where these strangers' home base is? Where do they fly from?"

The girl looked doubtful. "We're sure only that it's somewhere beyond the Rim, where we used to live."

That much, too, he had guessed. Dworn subsided into glum silence, as Qanya impassively guided the machine on its way, covering distance at a surprising speed.

Then, even by the unaccustomed daylight, Dworn recognized first one landmark and then another, and knew they were approaching the spot where he had been trapped last night. A weird return, riding as master in the monstrous machine that had snared him!

As the great tilted rock hove in view, Dworn strained for the first glimpse of his abandoned vehicle. When he saw it, lying still overturned in the shadow of the boulder, he sighed in relief. Its door was ajar, where Qanya must have dragged him stunned from the machine last night ... but it appeared unscathed. The fear at the back of his mind, that scavengers might have happened on it—in which case they would have had it dismantled and carried away by now—was happily unrealized. For that he perhaps had partly to thank the enemy against whom he had sworn vengeance, the flying fiends who had decimated and terrorized the peoples native to this land....

"All right," he ordered. "Stop here!"

The walking machine crunched to a halt, standing almost over the beetle. Dworn looked at the spider girl, then, in irresolution.

In the pitiless daylight she was still piquantly beautiful, though her pale face was still smudged with the remnants of her ceremonial make-up and her eyes were veiled, withdrawn. Yes, she was even desirable.... Dworn put that thought determinedly out of his head. After all, she was an alien and an enemy; she had sought to make a doomed slave of him.

But now that her usefulness to him was over, he didn't know just what to do about her. The sensible thing would be, of course, simply to kill her. Somehow he felt that he couldn't do that. It was one thing to kill in the impersonal fury of machine combat, a different matter when the victim was helpless within your reach.... And he remembered that she *had* helped him escape.

He could command her to return to her people, to the tender mercies of the Spider Mother—who would know by now of Qanya's part in Dworn's disappearance. Damn it, that would probably be worse than killing her in cold blood! He was wasting time. Angry at himself for his unbeetlelike softness, Dworn postponed deciding what to do with her till he should have inspected his machine and made sure it was in shape to travel.

"Come along," he told the girl gruffly. "Outside."

Once more she obeyed unprotesting. The two clambered out of the belly of the standing spider—Qanya staring before her with sleepwalking fixity, Dworn nervously scanning sky and horizon for hostile machines. The sunlit waste was terrifyingly immense bright, and empty. With a physical ache of yearning he longed for the cramped security of his own machine's cabin.

He brushed past the girl and ran toward the upside-down beetle—he could easily right it with a spare emergency cartridge, and then he would be on his way in a normal world again—

He stopped short with one hand on the beetle's dull-black steel flank. The world seemed to rock around him.

The girl watched him without expression as his face went slack with horror, as he completed his arrested movement and dived into the cabin to confirm the dreadful discovery that first touch had disclosed to him.

When Dworn climbed out he was white and shaking. He took a few steps away from the beetle and sank weakly down on the sunwarmed sand.

"What's the matter?" asked Qanya.

He turned and looked dully at her. He had completely forgotten that she was there.

He said listlessly, "I'm *dead*."

"Of course you're dead." Her brows puckered faintly as she gazed at him. "Naturally, I drained your fuel tanks last night—"

Dworn surged to his feet and took one step toward her, fists knotted, blown by a gust of fury. She stared levelly back at him, unflinching—and he halted, shoulders drooping. "Ah, what's the use?"

He should have foreseen this—not that it would have done any good if he had. The beetle's fuel supply had been drunk up by the spider now towering over them; and the beetle's engine, even idling at minimum consumption, had used up what little remained in the system, and had stopped. And it was as if Dworn's own lifeblood had been drained and his own heart had stopped beating.

Qanya was still watching him blankly. She said, "Can't you start it again?"

Dworn was jolted by the realization that she genuinely didn't understand that he *was* dead—that there was no way of restarting an engine once stopped. Until now he had supposed that all races were the same in that respect; but evidently spiders were different. In fact, now he remembered that, when they had entered the spider-vehicle, the girl had pushed a button that apparently started the engine. Spiders, then, died and came to life again every day—a startling notion.

But the beetles—Among the thoughts that tumbled disjointedly through Dworn's head in this awful moment was a clear vision of the night, five years ago, when his machine-existence had begun: when, in the horde's encampment by the sea a thousand miles from here, the beetle's last seam had been welded, and its engine set going with the appropriate ritual of birth.... The sixteen-year-old boy's heart had beaten high and proudly, in tune with the heart of steel and fire that had begun to throb at that moment. And the life expectancy of the two was measured with the same measure, the life of flesh and that of metal indissolubly entwined....

He mumbled dazedly, "I'm dead, do you hear? Dead!"

There was a sudden howling in the sky. Flashing overhead, as the two stood momentarily petrified, went a shrieking flight of half a dozen winged shapes—stubby vanes slanting back from vicious noses, they hurtled low over the desert and vanished swiftly into the distance, dust-devils dancing across the ground in the whirling wind of their passage.

Dworn stared after them, and his eyes narrowed. A new and desperate resolve had begun shaping itself in his mind.

Of the things he had meant to do in life, it was no use thinking any more of rejoining his people. He was dead to them, for sure—not even a beetle any more, but only what was left of one, a ghost.... But a holy duty, stronger than death, remained to him; his father was still unrevenged.

What he could do against a foe so powerful as those who had just passed over, he had no idea—but perhaps a ghost could accomplish what a living man might well deem impossible.

He motioned Qanya peremptorily toward the waiting spider-machine. "Come on. We're taking your machine, and we're going to find *them!*"

For a moment she seemed to hesitate ... then she obeyed. If her face was paler than usual, Dworn failed to notice it.

The spider-vehicle lurched and swayed, even its marvelous system of shock-absorbers protesting as it climbed steeply, straddling upward from rock to rock.

Dworn clutched at handholds inside the pitching cabin and tried to combat the sympathetic lurching of his stomach. Qanya huddled tensely over the controls, slim hands flashing nimbly to and fro as with incredible deftness she guided the laboring machine.

Dworn risked a glimpse from the turret-windows, then shut his eyes with a rush of giddiness. They were climbing now up the steepest part of the great slide, where the mountainside had collapsed in a chaos of splintered rock and tumbled crags that would have been utterly impassible for any wheeled vehicle. Below them, the sloping valley floor they had left appeared from this height entirely flat and sickeningly far away. And still the cliff-heads frowning above them seemed terribly remote.

"How ... far?" gasped Dworn.

"It can't be very far now to the top," said Qanya, without glancing up from her absorbed concentration. Both their lives were in her hands; a slip, a misstep, and they might fall hundreds of feet among the jagged rocks to their death.

For seconds at a time, the walking machine poised motionless, one or more of its clawed limbs groping for footholds. As it clambered painfully upward, it was hopelessly exposed to attack if it should be sighted from the air.

Dworn, the beetle told himself savagely, *you are not only a ghost, you are an insane ghost. Only a madman would have undertaken such a journey.*

The cabin heeled wildly as the machine grappled a ledge and, its engine panting at full throttle, levered itself upward a few more feet.

He had commanded the spider girl to find the route by which her people had descended. But twice already they had missed the way and had arrived at dead ends beyond which it was impossible to climb higher; twice they had been forced to descend and search for an easier path. It had been scarcely noon when they started; now the sun was already sinking low.

Dworn could not even be sure that he would find his sworn enemies beyond the Barrier. But the duty of vengeance was all he had left to live for, since what was to have been his triumphal return had ended in bereavement and catastrophe.

And a dead man, thought Dworn bleakly, *needs something to live for, even more than other people do.*

The world came level again, for the moment. The machine sidled precariously along a narrow ledge girdling an unscalable wall of rock, as Qanya sought a spot to resume the ascent. Dworn winced at the thought that the way might be blocked again. But, no—fifty yards further on, the wall was breached, and toppled boulders formed a perilous but not impossible stairway.

Just as Qanya grasped the levers which would set the spider scrambling upward once more, there was a sound—one grown hatefully familiar to Dworn since the night before, the feverish buzzing of a number of light high-speed engines. He opened his mouth to hiss a warning, but Qanya too had heard. Instantly she guided the spider-machine as close as possible to the cliff, where the hollowed rock afforded some shelter, and twirled a knob that made it sink down, legs folding compactly.

They waited scarcely breathing. A couple of times before they had huddled like this, while flights of the winged enemies whistled over ... but the wingless ones? It seemed impossible that they should be up here, where surely nothing that ran on wheels could travel....

The head of a column of the aluminum crawlers came into view, whirring along the ledge with a confident air of knowing where they were going. One by one, the little machines rolled past within a few feet of the crouching spider, hastening on with an uncanny pre-occupation.

Dworn saw that, like those he had seen earlier, they were of diverse kinds; and several of them, fitted with claws and racks for transporting booty, were heavily laden now with metal plates and girders carved from some larger machine, a roll of caterpillar tread, a slightly bent axle.... The last pygmy in line, whose afterbody was a bloated tank, gurgled as it jolted by, and trailed an aroma of looted fuel.

A few yards beyond the staring watchers, each of the little plunderers pivoted sharply in its turn and without even slackening speed vanished straight into the cliff-face. Dworn and Qanya looked incredulously at one another.

"A tunnel!" Dworn grunted in realization.

That explained one mystery, at least—how, if the winged and wingless strangers' home base was somewhere above the cliffs, the wheeled machines contrived to forage at the foot of the Barrier. They must have one or more inclined tunnels, bored through solid rock for a distance that staggered Dworn's imagination. Emerging at this level, they had found or constructed a passable road the rest of the way to the valley floor.... Now he noticed that the ledge to which the spider had so laboriously climbed showed signs of being an often-used trail, and the cliffs it skirted exhibited in places the raw marks of recent blasting.

"Remember this spot," he told Qanya. "If we should return this same way—there's evidently an easier path down."

She said nothing. Dworn wondered wrily if, in her drug beclouded mind, she was aware of how unlikely it was that either of them would be returning from beyond the Barrier.

A mad enterprise indeed—a ghost and a zombie, going to seek out a foe whose numbers and whose might grew ever more apparent. The tunnel opening here was clear evidence of engineering resources and skill far beyond that of any of the machine races Dworn knew.

Its discovery was no help to them, since it was far too small to admit the spider.

"Go on!" Dworn ordered doggedly. "At least we know now that *their* dwelling can't be far!"

Qanya glanced briefly sidelong at him, then moved the levers, and the spider rocked upright once more and began to climb.

The sun was low, and the shadows of rocks and dunes in the valley behind them were pointing long blue fingers eastward, when the machine staggered up the last precipitous ascent and stood on level ground at the summit.

Dworn took a deep breath and looked ahead, looked for the first time in his life upon the unknown land beyond the Barrier.

At first glance, it differed little from any of the desert country where he had lived all his life. The ground shelved gradually away from the rocky rim on which they stood; far off, against the darkening eastern sky, blue mountains rose murkily, but between here and the ranges lay a vast shallow depression, an arid sink floored with wind-rippled sand. Perhaps it had been a lake-bed once, before natural or unnatural cataclysms, and the millennial drying-up of all this country, had emptied it of water. Or perhaps—as its circular form suggested—it was one of those other, mysterious depressions which were scattered irregularly across the face of the earth where no lakes had ever been; those, legend said, were scars left by the ancients' wars.

The rich light of the declining sun fell at a shallow angle into the miles-wide bowl and brought out with startling clarity the maze of wheel-tracks, crossing and criss-crossing, which covered its sandy expanse and testified to a fever of recent machine activity there. The light gleamed, too, here and there, upon scurrying metallic shapes, that raced by ones and twos or in trickling columns to and from the center of the bowl, where—

Dworn strained his eyes and his capacity for belief in an effort to make sense of the structures there, miles away. He was not very successful, for the scene was too unlike anything he had ever looked on before.

There were certain races which built stationary dwellings—Dworn knew of the scale-makers who lived, in colonies sometimes of considerable size, beneath individual armored, anchored domes sunk into the face of some impregnable rock; he knew of the sand devils with their pits, and now he had seen also how the spider people nested. But the huge buildings that loomed yonder, lowering and windowless, and the winged things clustering thick on the ground about them, were such as he had never seen in his nomadic life.

Atop a slender tower that spired above the squat structures he could make out something which turned and turned, something like a broad net of lacy wires, revolving steadily from east to west, from north to south. Strange, too, the smooth-surfaced ways that radiated outward in four directions, like an immense cross, broad paved roads that came to abrupt dead ends a mile or more from the central buildings.... After a moment, though, he guessed that those were runways for the aircraft which flew from this place.

The unknown builders were obviously a mighty people, a people who had perfected their peculiar form of organization on a gigantic scale. And a people who acted and thought strangely; for their behavior, as Dworn had observed it, suggested a chilly-blooded and fanatic discipline, a regimentation which he found monstrous and repellent.

Dworn turned questioning eyes on Qanya.

"I don't know what they are," she answered his unspoken query in a voice that faltered. "I remember this valley. But a few months ago it was uninhabited. All this has been built since then."

Dworn hesitated. He was seeing very clearly now just how hopeless this mad expedition was. Nevertheless, he had sworn vengeance, and he could at least perish with honor.

But—Seeing the fear in Qanya's face, it came to him sharply that, after all, she had no part in his blood feud. She had served him well by bringing him this far. The vague plans he had had, of using the spider-machine for an attack on the enemy, stood revealed as rankest folly. Big and powerful as the spider was by ordinary standards, against such as those it could accomplish little more than a man with his bare hands.

Which was what Dworn would be—He stifled further reflection, said crisply: "You can go now. I'll remain here; I have a duty to perform. But you can return—go make your peace with your people, or whatever you like."

Qanya's black eyes met his squarely. "I won't," she said.

"Now see here—" Dworn began, and broke off, thunderstruck.

"B-but," he gulped, "you *can't* disobey me. The drug, the spider poison—"

"Doesn't work on a born spider. I must have neglected to mention that, naturally, *we're* all immunized against it." She smiled with a flash of those sharp white teeth.

"Then—then—" Dworn stumbled, feeling his preconceptions tossed helter-skelter. "Then you must have come with me—of your own free will!"

"At first," murmured Qanya, "I knew you'd never trust me unless I pretended ... and I was curious, too, to see how it was to be the one that obeyed. And then ... well, you'd have known, if you'd ever seen how the drug really works. You should have realized, anyway, when I laughed at you.... But you do so love to be masterful don't you?"

For a moment, Dworn's chief emotion was one of quick rage at the revelation of how thoroughly she'd deceived him. Then the anger subsided and left him feeling merely foolish, as he saw that she'd merely let him deceive himself. And, finally—as it came home to him that this girl had followed him of her own choice into exile and great danger—a new and quite unaccustomed feeling flooded in on him, a queer sense of humility.

"I'm sorry," he said confusedly. "I didn't—I don't—understand."

She breathed in a barely audible voice, "You said I was beautiful.... And *you* hadn't the drug."

From far away, from around the vast, mysterious buildings, came mournful hooting sounds, a sighing and a sobbing as of some mythical monster in torment.

Dworn was rudely recalled to realization of where they were—and of the fact that, as the spider-machine stood poised here on the cliff-edge, it would be starkly visible from over there, seen against the setting sun.

He gave up trying to unsnarl the tangle of his own feelings. He said hurriedly, "But you should go back. There's no time—I *have* to go on. But there's no reason you should die."

Qanya's face was drawn and determined. "No," she said flatly.

"I don't know what you're talking about. But I won't leave you now...."

The distant sighing rose to a whining roar.

"Quick!" cried Dworn in desperation. "Find cover. I think we've been seen!"

The girl reached for the controls and the spider's engine raced up. But it was already late. Off yonder, along that one of the radiating runways that stretched toward them, something was moving, racing swiftly and more swiftly outward with its long shadow following it.

All at once the moving thing left its shadow behind, and Dworn recognized it for an aircraft taking off.

Then he had to snatch for a handhold as the spider-machine lunged into a dead run. At full speed on the level ground, it could make good time; the ground outside skimmed past at fifty or sixty miles an hour.

Qanya had spied some rocky outcroppings, which might furnish a modicum of shelter, about a mile away and some distance from the brink of the cliffs, and she was heading for them. But the terrain nearer at hand was implacably flat—and the enemy was airborne, a vicious winged shape growing at terrifying speed. Its whistling roar swelled and grew deafening.

Qanya shouted something inaudible and pointed. Dworn understood, and, holding on for dear life in the pitching cabin, clawed his way within reach of the fire-controls. Wrestling with the unfamiliar mechanism, he fought to train the spider's guns on the hurtling attacker.

Puffs of smoke bloomed high in air—but any hit on such a fast-moving target, from so unstable a platform, would have been a miracle. The enemy screeched overhead, and an instant later flame and thunder erupted all around the running spider. The machine stumbled and for a moment seemed going down, but it righted itself and staggered on.

Dworn shook his ringing head and saw the flier banking steeply half a mile away, while a second and a third were climbing against the sky, gaining altitude to dive.

They couldn't last another thirty seconds, couldn't even hope to reach the doubtful cover of the rocks.... Up ahead, two hundred yards, was a low mound, only a few feet high, the only nearby elevation of any sort. And it was plainly artificial, though wind-piled sand had softened its outlines; others like it were scattered around the periphery of the great sink, and Dworn guessed their nature as he saw a column of the aluminum crawlers beginning to emerge from the side of the one just ahead. It must be the other end of a tunnel such as they had discovered among the cliffs....

He nudged Qanya urgently, shouted, "Head for that!"

She gave him a fleeting, wide-eyed look. The mound's low swell could furnish no shelter for the towering spider, and the tunnel mouth was of course much too small to enter. But she veered without slackening speed in the direction indicated.

Dworn abandoned the useless guns. The mound, with a gleaming line of crawlers still parading out of it, swept closer; and at the same time the desert echoed back the screaming onrush of the two new attackers.

Dworn wrenched open the cabin door with one hand. His other arm circled Qanya's waist, dragged her away from the controls. She cried in uncomprehending shock as he swung her before him into the open doorway. They swayed there, high above the speeding ground, wind whipping at them as the spider pounded blindly on.

The mound loomed immediately at hand. Dworn prayed that he had judged the moment right, and with a mighty leap launched both of them out into space.

A pistoning steel leg barely missed them. Even as they fell, the air was torn by explosions as the swooping fliers opened fire.

Dworn hit the ground with almost stunning force. His hold on the girl was broken and he was rolled helplessly over and over by his own momentum. But he fetched up on hands and knees, bruised and breathless but unhurt.

From the corner of his eye he saw Qanya sitting up dizzily, half-buried in the drifted sand that had broken their fall. Apparently she too was uninjured, but she was staring in horrified fascination after her runaway machine.

The spider careened onward, no hand at its controls. It hit the line of crawling little machines coming from underground; it knocked one spinning end over end, and stepped squarely on another, stamping it flat. It recovered its balance amazingly, and loped on, even though one leg was buckling beneath it—

Then it was hit dead-on by what must have been at least a hundred-pound high explosive rocket.

The winged killers shot low overhead with an exultant whoop of jets, peeling off to right and left of the column of smoke that rose and towered where the spider had been struck. Out of the cloud, metal fragments soared glinting upward and arced back to earth, and on the ground, amid smoke and dust, a metal limb was briefly visible, flexing convulsively and growing still.

Dworn heard a smothered sound beside him. A tear rolled down Qanya's smudged cheek, and Dworn thought fuzzily, *Even spiders can cry. Only*, he corrected, *she's not a spider any more she's now just a ghost like me.*

If he hadn't been a ghost already, if he hadn't lost his own machine—
the idea of jumping clear and saving both their human lives while letting
the spider be destroyed would never have occurred to him.

He came to himself, hissed, "Down! Keep low and maybe they'll
overlook us!"

They huddled together on the slope of the sandhill, while the victorious
flying enemy circled round in a miles-wide sweep and began descending
toward their base again, wing-flaps braking them for landing.

And on the ground meanwhile, the crawlers which had come from the
tunnel were proceeding on their way, leaving two of their number behind
with strange indifference to their own casualties.

"What'll we do?" quavered Qanya.

Dworn had time to take stock of the situation. The tunnel-mound was, as
he had seen before, the only cover—and that a poor one—for a considerable
distance. It was all of a quarter mile to the edge beyond which the cliffs fell
away.

He tried to sound hopeful—whether for Qanya's sake or to keep up his
own courage, he could hardly have said. "I think we'll have to stay here,
and hope we're not noticed, until it gets dark. Then, maybe—"

Qanya caught her breath sharply and gripped his arm. "Look—there!"

Still far away across the sloping floor of the great bowl, but rapidly
approaching from its center, moved a dust cloud. Beneath it, the expiring
sunlight glinted on the aluminum shells of at least a score of the ground
machines.

Dworn said grimly, "Might have expected it; they'll be coming to look
over the scene of action and pick up the pieces. We've one chance; keep out
of sight behind this little hill, and maybe they won't investigate too closely."

Qanya nodded, biting her lip. She could reckon as well as he how much
that chance was worth.

The buzzing motors came nearer. The two cowering in the lee of the
mound, almost without daring to breathe, heard them halt, slow to idling
speed one by one a little way off, where the wrecked spider lay. From that
spot obscure sounds began rising, thuds and gratings and a shrill hissing
noise.

But then—the whine of a single high-speed engine rose again, clear to
their hearing. One of the enemy was approaching around the flank of the
sandhill.

They crouched motionless, frozen. No hope in either flight or fight; on the open ground, they would be run down in no time, and they had no weapons—even the notion of a weapon, as something apart from the fighting machine that carried it, was alien to their thinking.

The enemy vehicle rolled into full view and nosed slowly along the base of the mound; its motor whining questingly, only a few yards of gentle slope between it and the huddled pair. Its vision-ports glinted redly in the sunset glow, and Dworn could almost feel the raking of murderous eyes from behind them.... Like the other machines of this kind he had seen it was small and without armor—it couldn't weigh more than a couple of thousand pounds, and it carried no guns. From the vantage of his armed and armored beetle, he had regarded its like as flimsy and harmless-looking.... But now he realized for the first time how helpless a mere human was against such a thing, and, with an irrepressible shudder, how easily the grappling and cutting-tools this one was equipped with might be employed for—dismantling—flesh and blood.

The machine paused momentarily. Then its engine revved up again. It rolled on past, giving no sign of excitement, and vanished beyond the hillside.

"Dworn, Dworn, it didn't see us!" Qanya was sobbing with relief.

Dworn was staring after the enemy, brows puzzledly drawn downward. The sounds from the other side of the mound went on uninterrupted—a clangor of metal, the prolonged shrilling of a cutting-torch, where evidently they were at work breaking up the smashed spider-vehicle.

He said huskily, "Something's very queer about them.... Wait. I've *got* to take a look."

Qanya glanced at him in quick alarm as he started wriggling to the crest of the sandhill. Then she followed silently, and peered over the top beside him.

Twilight was descending, but they could still see easily enough what went on out there. Not a hundred yards away, the little machines swarmed about the spider, bringing their various wrecking equipment into play to dismantle it rapidly under the watchers' eyes. Torches flared, winches tugged at fragments of the shattered monster. An aluminum cylinder with a serrated alligator snout rolled triumphantly away, bearing aloft the shank of a great steel leg....

But Dworn's attention was riveted by what was happening closer at hand. Here, near the tunnel-entrance that opened just below their observation point, lay the two crawlers which the runaway spider had disabled. One of these, the one which had merely been overturned and severely dented, was already being dragged away, wheels still helplessly in the air, by a towing-machine. The other had been smashed beyond repair. Around it several of the new arrivals were busy, callously and efficiently beginning to take it apart.

Dworn watched them at it, and the dreadful suspicion that had budded in his mind ripened into a monstrous certainty.

Aluminum skin was swiftly stripped away; frame members of the same metal were clipped neatly asunder by a machine armed with great shearing jaws. The engine came loose and was hoisted aloft carried dangling away by another specialized machine. In an incredibly short time, little but a bare chassis remained, and that too was being attacked by the salvagers.

And Dworn knew at last beyond all doubt, what manner of things these were.

Beside him he heard a sharp gasp, and turned to put a warning finger on Qanya's lips. He drew her gently back with him, out of view of the activities on the farther side of the mound.

"You understand what *that* means?"

The girl nodded soberly. "We have the tradition. I think that must be one tradition that all the peoples have in common."

"Then you know what we have to do."

She nodded again.

Between them the word hung unspoken—a word not to be uttered lightly, so awful was it in its connotations, freighted with memories of a terror rooted in the youth of the world.

Drones.

In the beginning—said the stories—there were the ancients, who were great and powerful beyond the imagining of the latter-day peoples. But the ancients were divided among themselves, for some of them were good and some of them were evil.

So they fought one another, with the terrific weapons of devastation which they owned. And the good triumphed in the end, as it must—though at terrible cost, for in those wars the earth was stripped almost lifeless; searing flame, plague, climatic convulsions wiped out the varied life which once populated the world, and finally there remained only the peoples of the machine, all of whom—diverse though their ways of existence had become, and for all that they lived in ceaseless conflict with each other—were descended from the victors in that primal struggle of men like gods.

But the evil old ones, though they were vanquished and their seed utterly annihilated, had nevertheless found a way to perpetuate their evil upon the earth. For before the last of them died, as a final act of vindictive atrocity, they created the drones....

Qanya was shivering uncontrollably. She whispered, "No one remembers when they last came. Some thought there were none left in the world."

"It's the same among my people," Dworn said hushedly. "There's no record of the drones' having appeared in the time of anyone now living.... But here they are."

From out of sight came the rattle and clank and whine of machines at work. And from farther away, from the direction of the great windowless buildings, there were hootings and throbbing sounds, and from time to time a deep rumbling that shook the earth.

Those noises were somehow unspeakably horrible now—now that they knew there was no one there. No one—nothing but the machines, without feeling or thought, without life, with only the blind meaningless activity of unliving mechanism set in motion and made self-subsisting a thousand or two thousand years ago....

With infinite caution the two humans peeked once again over the summit of the mound. Out there on the flat, the little wingless drones buzzed to and fro with their false seeming of animation, finishing their work.

From around the great buildings, whose interior no living eyes had ever looked upon, lights winked oddly blue through the thickening dusk. They caught glimpses of immense moving machinery, and heard mysterious sounds. Once and again, it seemed that in the open space before the structures a great door opened in the earth, and against a blue light that streamed upward they saw a vast winged shape rise majestically from underground and roll slowly forward into the shadows to join others already ranked there.

"What are they doing?"

"I don't know...." Dworn reflected, grasping at memories of the legends, the traditions he had heard. What he recalled was ominous. "I think I can guess, though. I think they're getting ready to swarm."

Her stifled exclamation was sign enough that she understood.

If the guess was right, the danger was on the verge of being multiplied many times over. Soon now, a swarm of queen ships would take to the air and fly in all directions, sowing the seed of the robot plague broadcast far and wide; one such colonizing vessel, no doubt, had founded this great hive only a few months ago. The things worked fast....

And Dworn's duty, and Qanya's, became all the more clear and urgent. Duty to spread the warning, at whatever risk to themselves. In the face of that, Dworn's mission of personal blood vengeance became unimportant—even if it had been possible to take such vengeance upon a foe with no life to forfeit.

He whispered to Qanya, "The ground machines are about to leave. When they're gone, we'll have to make a break for it." For some reason, as he pondered the distance they must cross to reach the Barrier cliffs, he recalled the strange revolving thing atop the central tower off yonder, turning constantly with its air of restless searching.... He swallowed painfully, repeated, "*Have* to."

The girl nodded silently. Impulsively Dworn put his arm around her; she pressed close against him. They huddled together like that, finding in one another's living warmth some measure of encouragement against the terror of the falling night in which nothing moved but the lifeless machines.

They watched while the lights glimmered far off across the flats; while a flight of fighter drones took off from there and howled away into the dark on some roving patrol; while, at last, the salvaging machines finished their work and rolled loot-laden away one by one.

More than once while they waited, other columns of the wingless drones entered or emerged from the tunnel mouth at the base of the mound. The tempo of activity in the hive was, if anything, increased as night came on. In the deepening darkness a faint blue glow streamed from the tunnel mouth.

As the whirring of the last salvager receded, Dworn got cautiously to his feet. He said between his teeth, "We'd better move fast, now—"

"Wait," said Qanya tensely. "They'll sight us in the open, and then what chance will we have?"

Dworn tried to make out her expression, but in the darkness her face was only a white blur. "We've got to try. There's no other way."

"Perhaps there is. What about the tunnel?"

Dworn was brought up short; that idea hadn't occurred to him at all. He said slowly, "I see what you mean, It's only big enough for one-way traffic—and the drones evidently have some system of remote control, so that outbound expeditions aren't using it at the same time as returning ones...."

"So, if we wait till some of the wingless ones enter from this end, and hurry through the tunnel close behind them—" Qanya left the sentence uncompleted. Dworn knew she could imagine as well as he what would happen if they failed to time it right, and met a drone column coming from the opposite direction. Still, the sound sense of the girl's ideas was obvious.

"All right," he said. "We'll try it that way."

It was another nerve-fraying wait until a file of ground machines came winding near and vanished one after another into the tunnel.

The two watchers gave them a little time—not too much—to get clear of the entrance. Then Dworn clasped Qanya's hand tightly in his own, and together they plunged down the sliding slope of the sandhill. The tunnel mouth yawned in its side, the bore on which it opened slanting steeply down into the earth, inwardly lit with eery blue light.

Hearts pounding, they raced into the tunnel.

It was an unreal, nightmare flight. The blue shaft curved and descended endlessly. Endlessly ahead of them echoed the snarling of drone engines.

They ran with lungs near to bursting, through air heavy and foul with exhaust gases—trying frantically to keep close behind that engine noise, while it receded inexorably before them. And once and again, amid the tricky tunnel echoes, Dworn was almost sure that other drones had entered and were descending the narrow way behind them, and before his eyes flashed hideous visions of the two of them overtaken and run down, here where there was scarcely room to turn, let alone fight or hide.

The featureless walls were pressing inward to crush them, swimming before eyes filmed with exhaustion, in the blue shimmer which no doubt sufficed for the perceptions of the drones but which hardly served human vision....

The tunnel was in fact perhaps a thousand yards long.

But it seemed as if they had been staggering for a lifetime through the nightmare, through the blue glow, and it scarcely seemed real when a patch of night sky showed through the exit before them, and when they stumbled panting out into the clean cold air of the mountainside, and saw the white radiance of moonrise over the Barrier cliffs above them.

They sank down to catch their breath on a rock not far from the tunnel. They'd made it none too soon—only a minute or two had passed when the night once more buzzed with motor noise, and a column of foraging drones rolled up the trail and plunged at full speed into the mouth of the shaft.

Qanya buried her face against Dworn's shoulder.

"Easy, now," Dworn whispered, patting her with clumsy gentleness. "The worst's over. We made it ... Qanya, darling, we made it!"

She looked up at him and by the moonlight he saw her smile tremulously. She said breathlessly, "Would ... would you mind saying that again, please?"

The moon was already high as they trudged across the rolling desert beyond the foot of the great landslip.

After the tunnel, the rest of the descent had been relatively easy; they had followed the trail used by the wingless drones, being forced off it only once by the passage of a cavalcade of the little marauders. And they had discovered, to their surprise, that the human physique—inferior though it might be to machines in ruggedness, speed, and other respects—was better equipped for traversing rough terrain than the most ingenious vehicle ever constructed.

But both of them, unaccustomed as they were to walking on their own feet, were dead weary. They tramped on doggedly, searching the shadows, hoping to come upon some living machine-creature—of what race, didn't matter now.

So far they had seen only abundant evidence that the drones were abroad in force tonight, preparing perhaps for their swarming time. Drones in the air and on the ground, and once the burnt-out shell of an unidentifiable machine with a crew of the wingless salvagers worrying it, and once the light of fires afar off where the winged ones had made a kill....

Qanya stumbled, and Dworn caught her round the waist as she swayed.

"Tired," she gasped in a little girl's voice, then stiffened her back with a resolute effort.

"We'd better rest—"

"No," she said shakily; and then abruptly: "*Listen!*"

Not very far away, lost somewhere among the tricky moon-shadows, there was a stealthy crunching. It was coming nearer.

With instinctive caution the two hugged the pool of shadow beside a boulder.

"Spiders!" Qanya recognized them first.

They came prowling out of the shadows, crunching rhythmically across an open moonlit space towards a hollow beyond. One, two, four of them, moving with furtive caution through the perilous night.

They had to be intercepted, the warning given. But it was a critically dangerous moment—suspicious and on edge, they might fire at the first movement they saw.

"Stay here," said Dworn shortly. He thrust Qanya back into the shadows, and walked steadfastly out into the clear moonlight, in the path of the walking spider machines.

He raised one hand on high, palm outward in an immemorial gesture that he could only hope would be seen. He shouted at the top of his voice, "Stop! Don't shoot! I come in *peace!*"

His heart leaped. The leading spider ground to a halt, and the others behind it. He saw a dim figure move atop the foremost towering machine; and before he could speak again, heard the rasping voice of the Spider Mother herself.

"You! The one who got away—and who seduced one of *us* from the ways of her ancestors—? What peace can there be between you and us?"

"I bring," cried Dworn clearly, "warning of the Drone."

There was stunned silence.

Dworn sensed the other spiders watching from the height of their machines; and he guessed something of what must be going on in the mind of the fierce old woman staring down at him. She would be wondering if an alien, a mere beetle, would be so far without honor, so anxious to save his own skin, as to lie in such a matter.

Then he felt Qanya's hand in his, and heard her cry out, her voice vibrant and assured: "It is true, Mother! I have seen them too. The night-fliers, the raiders—they are the evil things our legends tell of!"

The great machine took two steps forward and knelt low to the ground. "Come here!" rasped the Spider Mother, and when the two advanced till she could look into their young faces—"You swear to this?"

"We swear!" they said at the same moment.

The Spider Mother's face was like iron. She looked from one to the other slowly.

"Then," she said stiffly and formally, leaning over to extend a wrinkled hand to Dworn, "let there be peace between us ... between me and mine and you and yours, and among all living peace ... till the evil is no more!"

Dworn took the hand, and answered, hurriedly recalling ancient custom: "Till the evil is no more!" And heard Qanya echo the words.

All night the desert was stirring, with a feverish hastening of messengers. These were at first spiders—then, members of a half dozen, a dozen other races, as the word was passed from one people to another—as tribe after tribe of hardbitten, suspicious warriors, fingers, fidgeting on triggers at the open approach of their hereditary mortal foes, heard and were electrified by the news—

The Coming of the Drone!

And hand gripped hand, all feuds were forgotten, the peoples mingled in a common effort of hurried mobilization. The desert land below the cliffs crawled with them, a mixed multitude of constantly increasing numbers, girding themselves for war.

Ferocious predatory machines—spiders, wheel-bugs, scorpions— formidable in their armor and bristling with guns, lay alongside the more pacific slugs and caterpillars and snails which in ordinary times were their natural prey, and were freely fuelled and provisioned out of the stores which normally their possessors would have fought to the death to safeguard against the despoilers....

In the presence of the drones, there were no more natural enmities. For the drones were the Enemy. Their coming meant that all life was kindred; deep in the heritage of every people was the almost instinctive knowledge that, if the drones were not checked as tradition decreed, their blind automatic propagation would end by sweeping every living thing from the face of the Earth.

Toward morning, the chiefs of a score of tribes held council of war in the very shadow of the Barrier. Their consultation was brief; there was no arguable question of what must be done, only of how. And if the drones were about to swarm, they must act promptly. No time to wait for the gathering of more distant peoples; no time to send word to the wasps or the hornets and gain aerial support. They must strike with what they had.

Dworn started awake as a hand touched his shoulder. He sat up, angrily flinging a coverlet from him.

"I didn't intend to sleep!" he muttered, rubbing his eyes and realizing where he was—below ground in the spiders' colony, whither he and Qanya had been taken and where he had been persuaded to lie down and rest a little while the warning was carried by others.

The tall blonde spider, Purri, was grinning maliciously down at him. "Hear the beetle talk! I suppose, after a day spent in what, for you was comparative idleness, you felt like doing something really strenuous ... say going out and demolishing the drones' hive bare handed...?"

Dworn climbed to his feet. With a violent effort he kept from wincing at the protest of stiffened muscles and yesterday's collection of bruises.

"What's going on out there now? Where's Qanya?"

"There's really nothing more *you* can do, you know. I merely woke you because I thought you'd want to hear that your beetle-folk have been contacted—they'd holed up to lick their wounds about twenty miles south of here—and have joined the fighting force that's getting ready to attack the drones at dawn. As for dear little Qanya, she's sleeping angelically in the next chamber...."

"No, she isn't," said Qanya from the doorway.

"You, too?" said Purri with irritation. "And what do you want, scapegrace?"

Qanya's black eyes narrowed dangerously. She moved forward to Dworn's side and took a grip on his arm. "I might ask what you're doing here disturbing—"

"Both of you, you're wasting time," growled Dworn.

He'd heard with a queer pang that his people—those who remained alive—had been located. Not that it made any real difference, of course. His father was dead, and he, Dworn, was dead too as far as his own kind was concerned. Nor, in this world, was there anywhere else he could turn.

For the present, under the threat of the Drone, that didn't matter. All laws of all peoples were in abeyance for the duration of the great emergency. But once the threat was dissolved, and the old laws resumed their force, the plight of Dworn and of Qanya also would be what it had been—that of outcasts in a world where an outcast had no chance of survival.

Well, it was no use thinking of the future. Dworn said determinedly: "I want to see the end of this business, at least."

"And I!" declared Qanya. "We've earned that right."

Purri eyed them sourly, shrugged. "As you like. I'm in command here while the Mother's busy at the front. I'll see you get transportation up there." Turning toward the door, she glanced sidelong at Dworn.... "You'll have to go separately, since a spider will only carry two. I'm leaving right away myself; *you* may come with me in my machine—"

"No, he won't," declared Qanya with finality, tightening her hold on Dworn's arm. "He can ride with old Zimka."

Purri stalked through the doorway before them, grumbling to herself, "Why is it the best ones always get away?"

Earlier in the night, climbing spiders—the only machines which could manage the ascent of the toppled Barrier—had scouted the periphery of the drones' fortress, and discovered the sole possible approach to it. At a single spot above the slide, a low ridge made it feasible to surmount the rim and steal out onto the table-land beyond without coming in direct view of the enemy's installations.

Once that was known, the council of chiefs decided on a daring strategy. Up the thousand-foot slope of tumbled rocks below that one vulnerable point, a fantastic supply line was established. One by one, machines from among those massing on the desert below toiled upward until wheels or treads could carry them no further; then they were hoisted bodily over the precipices by the invaluable spiders, who anchored themselves firmly in place with the powerful steel cables they ordinarily used for snaring prey, and used other such cables as pulleys.

Through the remaining hours of darkness the joined forces labored with Herculean devotion to accomplish the seemingly impossible task. There were brushes with the enemy, for the wingless drones still came and went about the mountainside and from time to time their winged kindred flew overhead. But strict orders had gone out to all the allied peoples—avoid opening fire, avoid precipitating a general engagement, and freeze motionless whenever the fliers passed over. This last instruction rested on the observation that the robot predators, with whatever sensory devices they used, apparently had difficulty in spotting anything but a moving target.

In this wise, when dawn began to break, close to three hundred first-line fighting machines of a dozen different species had been raised to the summit of the Barrier. Thence they filtered cautiously out across the plateau, in a great arc moving to enclose the hollow of the drones.

The sky was lightening when Dworn and Qanya settled themselves to watch from the crest of the rocky ridge which had shielded the attacking forces' deployment not far from the brink of the cliffs.

Behind them, the spiders which had brought them here melted stealthily away toward the east, going to take their places in the battle line.

The two were alone once more, looking out over the vast circular depression infested by the enemy, just as they had yesterday at sunset. But today, as the sun rose, the situation was very different. For miles around the circumference of the great hive, there were furtive stirrings, last-minute movements of preparation for the imminent assault. From behind every outcropping and fold of the ground, grim gun-muzzles pointed inward, ready to begin spitting fire when the zero second came.

From here the central buildings of the hive were plainly visible, standing out against the sunrise. Around them moved many of the tireless worker machines; and the parked aircraft seemed more numerous than they had been the night before. Among them a score or more of winged shapes loomed conspicuous for their great size; when you made proper allowance for the distance, you realized that they were immense.

Those would be the queens—loaded and ready to take flight on their one-way journey to found new colonies wherever their evil destiny might lead them. The time of swarming was near.

Dworn scowled darkly, squinting against the light in an effort to judge the enemy's numbers. He grunted, "I hope ..." and bit his lip.

"What's wrong?" said Qanya tensely.

"Nothing.... Only it would have been well if we'd had time to bring up more reinforcements. But don't worry—we'll smash them." He was a little surprised to note that he said "we"—and meant any and all of the machine-peoples, united now in a common cause.

Dworn was bitterly wishing at this moment that he had had his beetle-machine again, and had been able to take an active part. As it was, he didn't even know surely just where in the battle line the beetles had taken up their position.

A distant explosion, a single gunshot, rolled echoless across the flats. It was a signal. Even as the shell hit the ground close to the ranked drone aircraft, motors had begun to pulse and snarl all along the farflung line. The desert began to spew forth attackers. A motley horde of metal things, they darted, stalked, and lumbered from their lurking-places, and as they advanced to the assault the firing commenced in earnest, became a staccato thunder that blanketed but failed to drown out the beginning alarm-wail of a huge mechanical voice from the fortress of the drones.

The enemy was not slow to react. Almost as the first rain of projectiles smashed down among them, jet engines began howling into life, and some of the fighter craft rocked into motion, wheeling out onto the runways.

The encircling attackers well knew the peril of letting any of those pilotless killers get into the air. Shellfire was being concentrated on the airstrips, striving to block them, plow them up with craters.

A fighter drone came roaring out one of the runaways gathering speed and beginning to lift. Dworn followed it with his eyes, feeling sweat spring out on his forehead, repeating under his breath without conscious awareness of what he was saying: "Stop him, *stop* him—"

Then the enemy craft spun round in the air, belching smoke, came apart and spilled along the runway for a hundred yards. A second, coming close behind it, plowed into the wreckage of its comrade, rolled over and over and became a furiously burning pyre. That strip was blocked.

All round the central hive smoke and flame were rising in innumerable places, from the paved ways and from the open desert. On another launching strip, just visible through the mounting inferno, one of the big queen-craft had sought to take to the air, and had been knocked out by heavy shellfire. Now its upended and blazing hulk tilted slowly over and collapsed burying beneath it several of the little wingless workers. In all the confusion these still scurried hither and yon, oblivious to the bombardment, laboring frantically but futilely to clear away the debris. Their efforts were useless, while the rain of explosives from the tightening ring of assault forces continued adding to the ruin and disorder within the hive....

Dworn sprang to his feet for a better view. He hugged Qanya to him till she gasped for breath, shouted in her ear over the thunder of the barrage, *"We've got them!"*

Close to the ridge where they stood a line of many-wheeled monsters rolled past—scorpions, moving along the battle front and, whenever the thickening smoke up ahead revealed a target, halting to wheel round and discharge their heavy-caliber tail guns.

Dworn had never liked scorpions, but he watched these with heartfelt approval.

Then he stared, bewilderedly aware that something had gone wrong. The big machines had turned and begun heading toward the ridge, clattering along at their top speed and no longer pausing to fire.

Within moments, Dworn perceived that all the other attackers were doing likewise; everywhere on the blazing battlefield, they had ceased their advance and were scattering to seek cover.

Only then, as the firing slackened, did he realize that the sky had begun to echo with a spiteful screaming of flying things. Against the brightening daylight hurtled some two dozen dark winged shapes ... fighter drones.

Dworn realized they must have been out on patrol, and summoned back by the drones' mysterious means of communication to defend the threatened hive. Now the flight was splitting into groups of two or three, diving to attack at one point and another and flitting away again so swiftly that human reflexes could scarcely act to train a gun.

Dworn glimpsed Qanya's horrified face beside him, and the girl threw her weight against him and dragged him down among the sheltering rocks. Overhead, from out of the sun, shot three of the winged drones. They passed over before the shrieking of their flight could reach the ears, and Dworn caught a glimpse of bombs tumbling earthward. Thunder crashed as the scorpions hugging the ridge threw up a vicious defensive barrage, and was drowned out as the bombs landed all around. The rocks heaved, and dust and splinters showered down from above.

Only a dozen yards away, a scorpion came rumbling up across the crest, its many wheels jolting over the rocks, and halted there, its tail gun weaving angrily as it sought vainly for targets in the sky. Along one of its gray-painted sides was a long bright gash where something had barely glanced from its armor. And Dworn saw, too, the black outline of a mythological arachnid on its observation turret, which signified that the machine belonged to a scorpion chief.

Scarcely knowing what he intended, he shook off Qanya's panic grip and plunged recklessly toward the big machine. As he scrambled over the rugged hilltop, he saw fleetingly what went on in the arena of battle—the allied peoples were being driven back, forced to concentrate their fire power on beating off aerial onslaughts. Meantime, the wingless drones about their beleaguered citadel worked feverishly to clear the way for their fighters that still remained undamaged on the ground.... Within minutes, unless something happened to turn the tide, there would be enough flying drones aloft to break the attack and inflict terrible losses.

Dworn found himself alongside the scorpion, just as its tail gun fired once more. The muzzle blast almost knocked him down, but he clawed his way up the side of the machine and began hammering on the observation turret hatch-cover.

"You in there!" he shouted. "Listen to me—"

The hatch cracked open and a grizzled head peered out, blinking at him with bewilderment and an automatic fierce suspicion. But at a time like this anything human was an ally.

"What's the idea?" demanded the scorpion.

The racket of gunfire and of jets made speech almost impossible. But Dworn pointed out across the sink, shouted: "Fire on the buildings—the central tower! They're controlled from somewhere—"

Luckily the scorpion leader—if that was who he was—was a man of quick understanding. He nodded vigorously and dropped out of sight again into the interior of his vehicle, bawling something to its driver. Dworn dropped off the machine's side as it lurched abruptly into motion. He watched, hardly breathing, as it slid to a halt at the bottom of the hill beside another of its tribe, and with shouts and gestures the word was passed on.

Inside a minute, all the nearby scorpions had begun banging away at the structures some three miles distant. The heavy scorpion guns were quite capable of carrying that far, and their shells had enough punch to do much damage to the buildings or to the central tower which still loomed occasionally visible through the drifting smoke....

But it was only a hope, perhaps even a forlorn hope. Dworn was fairly confident of his guess that the drones possessed some sort of central communication and control system—but it would take a lucky hit to disable that nerve center in time.

Qanya stumbled to his side. She cried something he couldn't hear over the continuous firing, tugged at him and pointed skyward with terror in her eyes.

The flying drones aloft had suddenly abandoned their scattered strafing attacks. With deadly machine-precision they wheeled into a single formation once more, and the whole flight came diving straight at the scorpion battery's position.

Dworn stood rigid, fists clenched at his sides, watching them scream nearer.

He ignored Qanya's pleading with him to take cover. No point to that— the drones' full force would blast the whole ridge to rubble and blanket it with their liquid flame.

At least, the enemy's reaction proved his inspiration correct. He noticed with fierce satisfaction that the scorpions were still doggedly firing....

The foremost drone came on, slanting down the sky until the gaping rocket-ports were plainly visible along its swept-back wings. But those sports still spat no flame. And it came on. It cleared the hilltop by no more than fifty feet, still diving faster than the speed of sound. It hit the desert slope beyond and ricocheted like a great projectile, bursting apart into fiery fragments that strewed themselves for a thousand yards across the rolling plateau.

Dworn picked himself up from among the rocks where he had been flung by the shock-wave of its near passage, and was knocked sprawling again by the earthquake impact of a second drone that thundered headlong into the earth a few hundred feet away, burying itself under a crater like that of a huge bomb.

He glimpsed a third craft going down to the west of them, just missing the rim of the Barrier cliffs and plunging out of sight without a sign of coming out of its dive.

Those which remained in the air were flying aimlessly. Two of them passed over side by side, gradually converging until, a couple of miles away, they locked wings and went spinning down toward the horizon in a deadly embrace.

On the ground, a like confusion had befallen the wingless workers. Their scurrying suddenly lost all its busy, planned efficiency. Some buzzed round and round in drunken circles; others ran head-on into one another, or tumbled into shell-holes to lie futilely spinning their wheels.

A hush descended on the field of battle. After the fury of bombardment and counterattack, the relative silence was deafening.

Dworn got to his feet for the second time and helped Qanya up; he grinned exultantly at her, oblivious of a trickle of blood running down his face where a rock-splinter had hit.

The scorpion lying nearest the foot of the slope opened its hatch-cover. A man climbed out, clasped hands together over his head and stamped on the gray monster's back in an awkward impromptu victory-dance. Cheers rang faintly from far off down the silenced firing-line.

Then—the spell of premature triumph was rudely shattered.

From the direction of the breached and smoking buildings, there rose yet again the soughing roar of jet engines gathering speed. Onto the runway to the west—the only one which the workers had managed to clear before their central control was knocked out—came waddling an enormous winged thing.

Its multiple engines screamed up to a frenzied pitch, and it rolled out along the strip at increasing velocity. Its huge wheels narrowly missed a dead fighter slewed across the way. Its tail went up.

Naturally, the queen ships wouldn't be dependent on the nerve-center of the hive that had spawned them; for each of them carried within itself the full-grown robot brain, the nucleus of a new hive....

Shooting began again raggedly, the gunners caught unawares. Perhaps the great machine was hit—but to stop it would take more than one or two hits.

It reached and passed the end of the runway, its wheels barely clearing the ground as the paved strip ended. Black smoke belched from its engines as it spent fuel lavishly, fighting heavy-laden for altitude. It rocked with the concussion of shells bursting all around it, and then it was soaring out over the Barrier, dipping and rolling perilously in the downdrafts beyond the cliffs. But it steadied and flew on, out of range of the guns, rising and dwindling until it was a speck, a mote vanishing into the western sky....

But no more queens escaped that day. The cannonade resumed with redoubled fury, and the guns did not fall silent until nothing was left to stir amid the gutted and blazing wreckage that had been the citadel of the drones.

Morning wind blew over the plateau, clearing away the reek of battle, bringing air that was cool and clear as it must have been in the morning of the world.

In that breeze like the breath of a new creation, it somehow seemed not at all strange to Dworn that he should be walking in the open under a daylight sky, among a multitude of excited strangers, men and women of all races, who mixed and exchanged greetings, laughed, shouted, slapped one another on the back ... then, perhaps, drew away for a moment with eyes of wonder at their own boldness....

Nor did it seem strange that Dworn strolled round the smoldering drone fortress hand in hand with a girl of the spider (who was by that token his hereditary foe,) and that he turned and kissed this enemy on the mouth, and she returned the kiss.

They stood with arms around one another, on the edge of the jubilant crowd, and looked out across the vast litter of smoking wreckage where scarcely a shell-holed wall stood upright now, from which the Enemy would no longer come to threaten the life of the Earth.

"One got away," said Qanya soberly.

"Yes. Somewhere it will all be to do over again." Dworn glanced toward the empty west, whither the queen flier had disappeared—where, perhaps, by now it would have crash-landed two or three hundred miles away, to spew forth its cargo of pygmy workers and (if the inhabitants or the area where it descended didn't discover and scotch it in time) to construct more workers, fighters, a hive no less formidable than the one that had perished today.

Dworn said, brow thoughtfully furrowed: "But maybe there's a good reason, even for the drones. Maybe they serve a purpose...." He faltered, unable to phrase the idea that had come to him—a thought that was not only unaccustomed but downright heretical. According to tradition the drones were the spawn of ancient evil and themselves wholly evil—but, Dworn was thinking, perhaps their existence produced good if, once in a generation or in ten generations, they came to remind the warring peoples that fundamentally all life was one in its eonlong conflict with no-life.

But he sensed, too, that that idea would take a long, long time to be worked out, to be communicated, to bear fruit....

Qanya's hand pressed his, and she said softly, "I think I know what you mean."

On one impulse they turned their backs to the ruins and gazed out across the throng of people, milling happily about, rejoicing, among the grim war-machines that stood open and abandoned on every hand. Near by, a crew of pill-bugs had tapped containers of the special beverage they brewed for their own use, and were inviting all passers-by to pause and drink.

"Your people are here somewhere," said Qanya. Her eyes on Dworn were troubled. "Over there to the south, I think I saw some beetles parked. Do you want to visit them?"

Dworn sighed. "Your people are here too."

"I know."

Neither of them moved. They stood silent, their thoughts the same; in a little while now, the Peace of the Drone would be over, and all this celebrating crowd would grow warily quiet, would climb back into their various fighting machines, close the hatches and man the guns and creep away in their separate directions. The world would go its way again, a world in which there was no place left for the two of them....

Dworn blotted the image from his mind's eye and bent to kiss Qanya once more, while the Peace lasted.

A voice called, "Dworn!" A familiar voice—one that couldn't be real, that must be a trick of his ears.

He turned. A little way off stood a small group of people watching them, and in the forefront was a stalwart man of fifty, in the green garment of a beetle with a golden scarab blazoned on his chest—

"*Father!*" Dworn gasped unbelieving.

They grasped one another's hands and looked into one another's eyes. Dworn was only dimly aware of the others looking on—among them the hard-faced Spider Mother, and the grizzled chief scorpion whose cohorts had struck the decisive blow in the battle.

Yold smiled with a quizzically raised eyebrow. "You thought I was dead, no doubt? You came on the spot where we were attacked and you saw—"

Dworn nodded and gulped. "I couldn't have been mistaken. I saw your machine there, wrecked.... And now I've lost mine." His voice trailed off miserably.

His father gave him a penetrating look. "I see. You're supposing that means everything is over."

"Doesn't it?"

The chief smiled again. "When you departed for your wanderyear, you were still a boy, though you'd learned your lessons and your beetle traditions well.... But now you're a man. We don't tell boys everything."

Dworn stared at his father, while understanding dawned like a glory upon him. To live again, the life he'd thought lost—

"So far as I could learn, your beetle was disabled through no fault of your own. In fact, by what these strangers tell me—" Yold nodded towards the Spider Mother and the scorpion chief—"you've proved yourself worthy indeed, over and above the customary testing. Of course, there will be the formality of a rebirth ceremony—which I have to undergo, too, so we can both do so together."

Dworn couldn't speak. Once again he had to remind himself that a beetle warrior didn't weep—not even tears of joy.

Then the Spider Mother spoke up, her voice brittle and metallic. "The girl will naturally be returned to us. After this business, I am going to have to take pains to restore discipline in the Family."

Dworn saw Qanya's desolate face, took one step to the girl's side and put a shielding arm around her. He felt Qanya trembling, and glared at the Spider Mother's implacable face.

"I won't go back!" Qanya cried vehemently. "I'll die first! I never wanted to be a spider, anyway!"

"And I," growled Dworn, "won't let you take her. I won't let her go—" his face was pale, but he went on resolutely—"even if it means I can't return to my own people."

The beetle chief surveyed the two young people gravely, then turned to confront the old woman. He said, "I don't see that you have any further claim on the girl. According to our customs, she too can be 'reborn'—this time into the beetle horde, as one of my people—and my son's."

The head scorpion, looking on, nodded approval and grinned encouragingly at Dworn.

The Spider Mother and the chief exchanged a long, stony look—on either side, the look of a ruler used to command.

"It would be too bad," said Yold softly, "to mar the Peace. But my warriors are within call, and...."

The Spider Mother turned away and spat. "Have it your way. Who wants weaklings in the Family!"

The chief glanced sidelong at Dworn and Qanya, and saw that they were wholly absorbed in one another. With an open-handed gesture he invited the Spider Mother to follow him.

"Shall we go, then," he suggested politely, "and—while the Peace still reigns—find out whether the pill-bugs' beverage is all they claim it is?"

www.ingramcontent.com/pod-product-compliance
Lightning Source LLC
LaVergne TN
LVHW041438170726
843492LV00008B/2672